Emily's House

Emily's House

BY *Niko Scharer*

PICTURES BY *Joanne Fitzgerald*

A Meadow Mouse Paperback
Groundwood/Douglas & McIntyre
Toronto/Vancouver

Canadian Cataloguing in Publication Data

Scharer, Niko, 1965-
    Emily's house

"A Meadow Mouse paperback".
ISBN 0-88899-158-4

I. Fitzgerald, Joanne, 1956- . II. Title.

PS8587.C432E5 1992   jC813'.54   C91-095448-8
PZ7.S35Em 1992

A Groundwood Book
Douglas & McIntyre Ltd.
585 Bloor Street West
Toronto, Ontario M6G 1K5

Design by Michael Solomon
Printed and bound in Hong Kong
by Everbest Printing Co. Ltd.

Emily lived in a little brick house
With a creaky old door and a little brown mouse.
Emily listened, and Emily frowned
'Cause Emily heard two very loud sounds!
For the door went creak
And the mouse went squeak
And Emily cried with a great big tear
And she said, "There's too much noise in here!"

Well, Emily sighed, "Oh what to do?"
But the mouse said, "Get us a pussycat too."

So Emily left in her white straw hat
And she came back home with a tabby cat.
And the door went creak
And the mouse went squeak
And the cat meow-ed
And meow-ed so loud
That Emily cried with a great big tear
And she said, "There's too much noise in here!"

Well, Emily sighed, "Oh what to do?"
But the mouse said, "Get us a puppy dog too."